# Disney's
# ENTER IF YOU DARE!

## SCARY TALES FROM
## THE HAUNTED MANSION

BY NICHOLAS STEPHENS

ILLUSTRATED BY
SERGIO MARTINEZ

Disney
PRESS

NEW YORK

# CONTENTS

# ENTER IF YOU DARE!

WELCOME, DEAR FRIEND,
   TO MY HUMBLE HOMESTEAD.
PLEASE TRY TO OBEY THE HOUSE RULES.
DO NOT PLAY WITH THE BATS
   OR DISTURB THE UNDEAD,
AND REMEMBER:
   DON'T HASSLE THE GHOULS.

PUT ASIDE ALL YOUR FEARS;
   FOLLOW ME IF YOU DARE,
AND I'LL TELL YOU SOME TALES,
   MY DEAR FRIEND.
JUST IGNORE THOSE LOUD SCREAMS,
   SIT RIGHT DOWN, TAKE A CHAIR,
AND WE'LL SEE IF YOU GET TO THE END.

# THE FORTUNE-TELLER

Y ou're the one who missed the pass," Joe
Lambert chided. "So go get the football,
Luiz."

"No way."

"Chill out. It's just a bunch of dead people."

"It's not the graveyard." Luiz Rodriguez lowered
his voice and glanced across the jumble of gray,
moss-covered gravestones to the house looming
just beyond. "It's the mansion next door. It's haunted. Everybody says so."

"No one's even living there right now."

"Why do you think people keep moving out?"
Luiz asked. "I've heard the stories."

Joe rolled his eyes. Luiz was so gullible. "That's
all they are—stories."

Suddenly a rasping voice called from the graveyard. "Does this belong to you, gentlemen?"

An old man, as gnarled and bent as the cemetery trees, approached slowly. Joe's football was in his hands.

"Thanks," Joe said gratefully, taking the ball and running his fingers over the signature inscribed on it. "My grandfather gave this to me. I'd really hate to lose it."

"It's my pleasure." The old man grinned, revealing a mouthful of rotting teeth. "Allow me to introduce myself. I am Ezekiel. I work for Madame Blackheart, who just moved into the big house there." He gestured toward the mansion.

"Really?" Luiz said, his eyes widening. "Not to be rude or anything, but I can't believe anybody would want to live there."

"Oh, Madame Blackheart doesn't just live there," said Ezekiel. "She works there, too. Madame is a seer—a fortune-teller. Perhaps you boys would like to come inside and see what the future holds?"

Joe grinned and grabbed Luiz by the arm. A trip inside the haunted mansion would make a great story to tell at school. "Come on. Let's check it out."

"No way. I'm not setting foot in there," Luiz said firmly. "I don't need to know my future."

"Just think," Joe said. "We can ask her if we really have to study for that math test tomorrow. We can find out if we're going to make the basketball team. The possibilities are endless!"

Luiz sighed. He knew Joe—he'd never give up until Luiz agreed to go with him. It was always the same. "All right, all right," Luiz said. "I'll go. But you owe me for this, man!"

Joe grinned. "Sure. No problem." He turned to Ezekiel. "Lead the way."

The two boys followed Ezekiel through the creepy old graveyard and up the rickety steps to the mansion. The huge door swung open with a low moan before Ezekiel touched the knob. A strange, musty odor hit the boys, the smell of dampness and decay.

They entered a dark, narrow hallway lit by a single flickering candle. Cobwebs hung like thick curtains from the ceiling, grabbing at the boys as they walked. From somewhere deep within the mansion came the low, eerie wail of a pipe organ.

"Wait here," Ezekiel instructed, shuffling away.

"It smells like my grandmother's attic in here," Joe said.

"It smells like something died in here," Luiz whispered back, clenching his fists nervously. "Did you ever stop to wonder who's in all those graves next to the mansion? I mean, how many houses around here have their very own private cemetery?"

Just then Ezekiel returned, smiling his ghastly smile. "Madame Blackheart will see you now."

He led the boys into a cavernous parlor. It was so cold they could see their breath form little clouds. Candles in a silver candelabra on the fireplace mantel cast deep shadows over the room. The only furniture was a table and one chair in the center of the room. On the table sat a round object a little larger than a basketball. It was draped with black velvet.

"I'll bet that's a crystal ball, right?" Joe asked Ezekiel.

Ezekiel gazed at the covered object. There was something in his eyes, something wild and terrified. "It is the source of all Madame's power," he whispered.

Suddenly he fell silent as a figure appeared out of the darkness. She wore an old-fashioned black dress and black gloves. A thick black veil shrouded her entire head. She looked as if she had been torn from the very night itself.

"You wish to see the future?" Madame Blackheart asked. Her voice was muffled and indistinct behind the thick veil.

"Maybe this isn't such a good time," Luiz said quickly, taking a few steps backward. He had a bad feeling about this. Joe's crazy ideas were always getting them in trouble, but this—this was really

creepy. "You're probably really busy, moving in and everything—"

"Nonsense. There is always time for the future." Madame Blackheart sat down. An icy wind tore through the room, extinguishing the candles on the mantel. The room was pitch black.

Luiz grabbed Joe's arm. "Let's get out of here," he hissed.

Startled, Joe dropped his football. It rolled under the table. "Hey, you're cutting off my circulation," he hissed back.

Suddenly a strange greenish glow appeared as Madame Blackheart lifted the black cloth partway off the round globe on the table. The eerie light played over her veil, creating weird shadows among the folds.

Joe wanted to get a look at the crystal ball. He'd never seen one before. But his feet seemed to have turned into thick blocks of lead.

"I shall begin," Madame Blackheart said. Murmuring and swaying, she peered at the round object beneath the black cloth. "One of you," she said suddenly, "shall grow to be a man of wealth and prominence."

"That would be yours truly," Joe said, elbowing Luiz.

"And the other"—Madame Blackheart's voice rose, becoming thin and shrill, like an icy wind—

7

"the other shall spend all of his days in an asylum for the hopelessly insane!"

Her voice hung in the air, stunning both boys into silence. Slowly Madame Blackheart lowered the black cloth, extinguishing the green glow. Darkness descended on the room once again. A moment later the candles flickered back to life.

Madame Blackheart had vanished.

Luiz headed for the door. "I am *outta* here."

"You read my mind," Joe said, sounding a little shaken. "That was pretty weird."

The boys charged down the hall toward the door, then burst out into the reddish late-afternoon sunlight. They ran through the cemetery, leaping wildly over the gravestones. They didn't stop until the mansion had disappeared from view behind them.

Luiz was just opening his math book that evening when the phone rang. He jumped at the sound, then grabbed the receiver.

"Luiz," Joe said. "We gotta go back."

"Back where?" Luiz asked, afraid of the answer.

"You know. The mansion. I left my football there, can you believe it? I guess I was sort of freaked out at the time."

"Yeah," Luiz said softly, recalling the ghostly image of Madame Blackheart drifting into the room. "Well, take my advice. Get another football."

"Can't do it. That's my genuine autographed Joe Montana. I gotta get it back. My grandfather gave me that ball."

"It's not a good idea, Joe. That Madame Blackheart is weird in a big way."

"Well, maybe we can find that Ezekiel guy and ask him to get it for us," Joe suggested.

Luiz shuddered at the memory of the strange, gnarled old man. "He's almost as freaky as she is. I don't want to have to see either one of them ever again."

"Come on, man," Joe pleaded. "We'll just sneak in and grab the football. They'll never even know we were there. Don't make me go back alone."

Luiz closed his eyes. Friends could be a real pain sometimes. "You're *really* gonna owe me," he said. "Assuming we live, you're gonna owe me *big*, Lambert."

A little after midnight the boys climbed the rusty iron fence that surrounded the mansion. The giant oak in the front yard swayed menacingly, grabbing for them with twisted, leafless fingers. The moon was just a pale thumbnail, but the gravestones in the cemetery seemed to glow with an unnatural light.

Joe and Luiz crept toward the big parlor window. The glass was cracked, the wood decayed and rotting. Standing on his toes, Joe could just reach it. He pushed on the frame and gasped. "It's open!"

"Sure it is," Luiz said. "It's not like there's anything to steal in there. Except maybe that crystal ball."

Joe eased the window open. It let out a low creak. "Give me a leg up," he whispered.

With a grunt of effort, Joe yanked himself up. Just as he straddled the sill, a dark, leathery hand slapped at his face.

Madame Blackheart! She'd discovered them!

A deafening squeal cut the air. Joe fell back, startled. He lost his grip on the sill and fell to the wet ground.

"It was *her*!" Luiz cried, getting ready to run.

"No, no," Joe said, sitting up carefully and trying to find his voice. "I think it was just a bat."

Luiz gazed up at the open window. It gaped like a black mouth waiting to devour them both. "Look, I'm having some major second thoughts here. How about if I personally buy you a new football? I'll have it autographed by the entire NFL—"

"Luiz, don't go wimping out on me again."

"I am not a wimp. I just have a weak stomach. It runs in the family."

Joe stood, brushing off his jeans. He swallowed past the tight dry spot in his throat. He had to admit, his own stomach wasn't feeling too great right now. But his grandfather had given him that football for his birthday, he reminded himself. His grandfather, who had died last summer. He *had* to get that football back.

"Give me another leg up," Joe said before he could change his mind.

This time he made it in without any trouble. He landed on the parlor floor with a loud thud. He waited—for voices, for movement, for more bats.

Nothing. He hadn't awakened anyone. Madame Blackheart must sleep like the dead, he told himself.

Okay, he added with a forced smile, so maybe that wasn't the best way to put it.

Gradually Joe's eyes adjusted to the dimness. There on the table was the ball draped in black velvet. And beneath the table he could just make out the outline of his football.

Joe took a few cautious steps forward. The floor moaned like someone in pain. He paused, holding his breath.

All he had to do was grab the football and make a run for it. Tomorrow he could tell everybody about his midnight visit to the mansion. Maybe he'd even spice things up a little—throw in a few ghosts and skeletons for good measure.

Joe reached under the table and grabbed the

football. It was already covered with sticky cob-webs. He brushed it off and tucked it under his arm.

Nothing to it, Joe thought as he stood. He turned to go, then paused, eyeing the object on the table. What would it be like to gaze into a crystal ball? Would it be like staring through a window, with nothing but the table on the other side? Or had Madame Blackheart actually seen something deep within that green-glowing sphere?

What did the future really look like?

Joe reached for the edge of the black velvet drape. He lifted it one inch, then two. The strange, sickly green glow began to pulse beneath the fabric. Joe bit his lower lip. Another few inches and he would be able to see what Madame Blackheart had seen, maybe even see through space and time.

Behind him there was a soft rustle of fabric.

Joe spun around, yanking the drape off the globe as he turned. Madame Blackheart was moving toward him through the pulsing, green-tinted dark-ness, moving slowly, steadily, moaning wordlessly beneath the folds of her black veil.

"I . . . ," Joe faltered. "I . . ." No words would come.

She moved toward him like a slow-motion nightmare, her black-gloved hands outstretched.

Behind him on the table, the green light

throbbed. But Joe couldn't take his eyes off the approaching figure. His knees were locked. He'd forgotten how to breathe.

The glow grew pulsating, brilliant.

He had to turn. He had to see.

Slowly Joe looked back, his feet still rooted to the floor. The glow was blinding. He blinked hard and looked again. There was something inside the glass ball.

Joe felt his legs turn to liquid. His stomach churned.

Inside the ball was a woman's head. Long flowing hair swirled around the pale green face and the ragged stump of a neck.

*It's not real*, Joe told himself desperately. *It can't be real!*

And then the head smiled. Its toothless black grin gaped at Joe, laughing a wild laugh that froze his heart.

Joe turned. Madame Blackheart was only inches away. With a terrible cry, she threw back her thick veil.

There was nothing there. No head. Nothing.

Nothing but a bloody stump.

The floor seemed to buckle and sway. Joe was dizzy. He was going to faint.

He dropped his football and grabbed for the table

as he fell. The rickety table tipped, and the glass ball began to roll toward the edge. A pitiful wail gurgled forth from the stump as the ball crashed to the floor and shattered.

Slowly the head rolled under the table. Madame Blackheart's headless body slumped to the floor.

As consciousness faded away, Joe reached for his football. He clutched it to his chest. But when he looked down, it wasn't his grandfather's football he saw.

It was the head of Madame Blackheart, the mouth frozen in a wild cry, the eyes flat and lifeless as they gazed up at him.

A week later Luiz paused in front of the mansion. It seemed to grin at him through black windowpane eyes, a hideous grin of triumph.

This was the first time he'd passed this way. He'd avoided this place ever since that night. The night of the terrifying scream, the night that Joe had . . .

But today Luiz was in a hurry. Visiting hours ended soon, and this route, past the mansion, was the quickest way. Clenching his fists in his pockets, Luiz hurried past, his eyes glued to the ground.

A raven called from the skeletal black tree in the middle of the cemetery. Luiz hesitated. He didn't want to look. But it was as if some power was forcing his gaze to the two fresh mounds of dirt beneath the black-limbed tree.

One was long. The size of a body.

The other was small. The size of a head.

There was only one headstone, at the end of the long grave. Against his will, Luiz read it.

RIP

HERE LIES
THE BODY OF
MADAME BLACKHEART.
THE REST IS
NEXT DOOR;
SEEMS IT GOT
A HEAD START

Luiz shuddered and turned away. If he didn't hurry, he'd be too late to visit Joe at the asylum.

# THE FACE IN THE MIRROR

J ust as it did every day, Sarah Janeway's alarm clock rang at seven o'clock. Just as she did every day, Sarah rolled out of bed and stuck her feet into her slippers. And just as she did every day, Sarah's mother called from downstairs, "Rise and shine! You don't want to miss the bus."

"Oh, but I *do* want to miss the bus," Sarah groaned. Then she brightened. At least it was Friday. Tomorrow she would be able to spend the whole day riding her horse, Turbo.

Sarah walked across the room, ruffled her brown hair, and smiled at her reflection in the mirror over her dresser, just as she did every day.

Only this day was different.

"Aaaaagh!" Sarah screeched, lurching back

16

against her bed. She fumbled with the covers and yanked the quilt over her head.

"I did *not* really see that," she said in a quivery voice. "I couldn't have. It wasn't real. I must still be asleep." She pinched herself hard on the arm. "Ow!" So it hadn't been a nightmare. Then what was it?

She waited until her heart stopped thudding in her ears. Then she pulled off the covers, emerging again into her familiar room.

Everything was as it should be. Her CD player was on her dresser. Her closet door was open, revealing the usual tangle of dirty clothes on the floor. And from downstairs came her mother's voice once again. "Sarah! Your breakfast is getting cold!"

Her hands clenched into tight fists, Sarah turned slowly, ever so slowly, to face the mirror again.

"Oh no. Oh no," she whispered. She could see the reflection of her lips as they moved.

And right beside her, grinning over her shoulder, she could see *him*.

The apparition's skin was gray green and wrinkled like an old, withered apple, although his eyes were terribly bright. A dirty, battered cowboy hat was jammed onto his head. His nose was smashed, smeared across his face, and his mouth grinned horribly, revealing a bloody gap where two front teeth were missing.

Sarah felt her flesh creep, a twitching, itchy sensation. She forced herself to stare, unblinking, at the mirror.

Yes. He was there, right there beside her.

Slowly she took a deep breath. Then, suddenly, she snapped her head around to catch him.

There was no one standing behind her.

*Of course there's no one behind me*, Sarah told herself. Behind her was the rumpled bed. Beyond that, the window. Her room, her things.

She slowly raised her eyes again to the mirror.

The horrible, mangled face was still staring back at her, its eyes glittering.

Sarah swallowed hard. "You're not real, you know," she told the apparition. "I just have a very active imagination. Everyone says so."

The apparition grinned his gapped grin, glaring with his neon eyes. Suddenly he pointed up and then ducked down out of sight.

To Sarah's horror, her own reflection began to change. The mirror showed her own nose smeared across her face, her own wide, screaming mouth now missing two front teeth.

She screamed again, loud and long, and fell back on the bed, gasping for air, her eyes closed to shut out the hideous vision.

A moment later her mother threw open the door and rushed in. "Sarah! Sarah! What's the matter?"

Sarah ran to her mother's arms and from their safety peered back at the mirror. All she saw was a terrified girl being comforted by her mother.

Sarah shook her head in horror and disbelief. "I . . . I guess I had a nightmare" was all she could manage to say.

On her way to school Sarah tried to forget the whole thing. The apparition obviously wasn't real. It was just some kind of strange waking dream. Maybe she should stop eating cold pizza before bed.

Josie Dobbs, Sarah's best friend, was waiting for her by the locker they shared. "Hey, Sarah, what's with your face?" Josie demanded, peering at her strangely.

Sarah's hand flew to her mouth. She remembered every awful detail of the mirror image, the smashed, bloody nose, the black gap where her teeth should have been. "What do you mean?" she cried.

"Get a grip, Sarah," Josie said. "I just meant you look pale. What did you think I meant?"

"Nothing," Sarah said quickly. "Pale? I guess I need to get out in the sun more."

"Yeah, you look like you've seen a ghost or something."

Sarah forced an uneasy laugh.

"Want to hit the mall tomorrow?" Josie asked.

"Can't," Sarah said. "I'm going riding." The thought of a day spent with Turbo made her brighten a little. Riding always took her mind off things.

Just above their heads, the warning bell for first period rang loudly. Sarah jumped and clutched a hand over her heart.

"It's just the bell, Sarah," Josie said, rolling her eyes.

Sarah fumbled with the combination lock on the locker. While she retrieved her books, Josie checked her face in the small mirror Sarah had attached to the door. "Hey, gorgeous," Josie said to her reflection, giving herself a pouty smile like a magazine model.

Distractedly Sarah took her own turn at the mirror. Every day she checked her face in the mirror before going to first period. And every day her face was pretty much the same.

Only this day was different.

The man with the terrifying withered face was there, right beside her in the small mirror.

"No!" Sarah cried, her voice thick with fear. As she opened her mouth to scream, she realized that her own nose was a smeared, bloody mess. Her two front teeth had vanished, leaving a black hole. Once again the man gave her a piercing stare, then ducked down and disappeared from sight.

"Oh, come on, quit playing around," Josie said.

Sarah clutched at her friend's arm. "Josie, tell me the truth. What do I look like?"

"Like the second prettiest girl in school."

Sarah tentatively raised one hand to her mouth. "Do I . . . do I have all my teeth?" she whispered.

Josie sighed heavily. "You know, you are *really* starting to get weird on me, Sarah. Now hurry up. We're going to be late."

As the day wore on, the apparition never left Sarah. In gym class he appeared beside her in the locker-room mirror, grinning his gruesome grin. Again Sarah's own face transformed into a reflection every bit as hideous, as the man pointed up and then ducked away out of sight. He appeared in the lunchroom when Sarah happened to look at Rob Gorsch, who was wearing a pair of mirrored shades. He appeared when she went to the girls' room to wash her hands.

By the time she headed for home, Sarah was a wreck. Obviously she was going crazy. She didn't feel crazy, but she supposed that was the whole point—crazy people didn't *know* they were crazy. What could she do? How could she possibly tell her parents? If she tried, her mother would just grin vaguely and say, *Oh, honey, you have such an active imagination.* Her father would frown and say something like *It's all the fault of that music you listen to.*

Back in her room at the end of the day, Sarah kept her eyes averted from the mirror where she'd first seen the apparition. She went to the hall closet and retrieved a sheet. Then, keeping her eyes squeezed shut, she draped the sheet over the mirror.

Sarah opened her eyes cautiously and felt a wave of relief. The mirror was completely covered.

"Now I can forget about this and get some rest," she muttered, staring at the sheet. She wanted to get an early start the next morning so she and Turbo could spend the whole day together.

Fortunately, there were no mirrors at the stable.

After a night of rain, the day dawned dark and cold. Thick gray clouds hung low in the sky, and the wind sliced through Sarah's windbreaker. As much as she'd been looking forward to riding, Sarah felt uneasy as she headed for the stable. She had tossed and turned half the night, disturbed by restless dreams. But in the morning she hadn't been able to remember any of them.

Before saddling up, she stopped by the stable

office to deliver the check her mother had given her for Turbo's boarding fee. In the office she found Ms. Shea, the stable owner.

"Thanks, Sarah," Ms. Shea said. "You'd better be careful out there today. It looks like we'll be getting some more rain."

Sarah opened her mouth to answer, but the words froze deep in her throat. She gasped, her eyes riveted to an old photograph hanging in a dusty corner of the office. It was *him*. She was sure of it. It was the apparition from the mirror . . . only different. Not frightening or deformed. Just a nice-looking man in an old-fashioned photograph, yellowed with age.

Ms. Shea followed Sarah's gaze. "I see you noticed Jake."

"Jake?" Sarah whispered, unable to tear her eyes away.

"Yep. That's the fellow who first built this stable, way back in the 1890s. Jake MacHeath. I'm surprised you haven't noticed that photo before."

Maybe I have, Sarah thought. Maybe I saw the picture without realizing it, and now it's stuck in my brain or something.

"Yep, old Jake had a colorful life," Ms. Shea said. "Fought in the Civil War, then bought this place. He's buried in the cemetery at that old abandoned mansion beyond the riding trails. You

23

know, the place over by Sedgwick Park."

Sarah swallowed hard. "How . . . um, how did he die?"

"I don't recall. Might say on his tombstone, not that I'd want to check it out. You won't see me setting foot on that property. Folks say the whole place is haunted, you know, and I'm not sure I don't believe them." Ms. Shea shuddered. "All I know is that the horses get a little spooky whenever they get near it. Animals know when something's not right."

Sarah felt an icy shiver sneak up her spine. She knew exactly which house Ms. Shea was talking about. The stables had miles of riding trails, but it was an unwritten rule that nobody rode anywhere near the far edge of the property that abutted the haunted mansion. Ms. Shea wasn't the only one who'd heard stories about it.

"Why is Jake buried there?" Sarah asked.

"Story goes he was in love with the widow of the mansion's original owner. I guess she's the one who had him buried there."

Sarah took one last glance at the photo, then left the office and headed for the tack room. So now her apparition had a name. Jake. Jake, a man who had been dead for almost a hundred years—and buried at the haunted mansion.

She tried to forget about all that as she let herself into Turbo's stall and greeted the big brown horse affectionately. She tacked him up and led him outside, casting a nervous glance at the sky, which looked darker than ever. "Looks like we may have a short ride today, boy," she told the horse. "Or a wet one."

Turbo just snorted in response. Sarah mounted, adjusted her stirrups, then rode out of the stable yard toward one of the wooded trails beyond. Turbo seemed more skittish than usual, and Sarah guessed that he was nervous about the weather. She knew that horses sometimes got that way just before a storm. *Animals know*, Ms. Shea's voice floated into her mind. *Animals know when something's not right.* Sarah shuddered, reminded once again of Jake's hideously deformed face—and, even worse, of the image of her own smashed nose and missing teeth.

Lost in her dark thoughts, Sarah allowed Turbo to choose his own way along the meandering trails. She didn't notice where they were heading until they'd already reached Sedgwick Park. The riding trail twisted along the edge of the overgrown park, then passed the grounds of the haunted mansion, which lay just beyond it.

"Oh man," Sarah muttered. "I'm really out of it."

She felt guilty for not paying closer attention to what she was doing—she knew that was an easy way to get hurt while riding. "Let's head back, boy," she told Turbo. "We can do some riding in the ring instead."

But just as she started to turn Turbo around, a black snake darted across the path. That was all the already-nervous horse needed. Turbo reared up in terror, hooves flailing, neighing shrilly.

"Quiet, guy, it's just a harmless little—," Sarah began, but just then her left foot slipped from the stirrup. She fought to maintain her balance, clutching at Turbo's mane as the reins slipped out of her grasp.

Suddenly the big gelding was off, tearing away at a full gallop. All Sarah could do was hold on and pray she didn't fall off and break her neck. The terrified horse jumped the fence of the empty park, landed heavily, and kept running. Thorns and brambles tore at Sarah's boots and sliced through her jeans. Beneath her the panicked horse ran jerkily, wildly, ignoring Sarah's desperate attempts to regain control.

About halfway across the park, the land rose slightly and there was a break in the trees. As she looked up, Sarah gasped in terror. Ahead of them, atop a barren hill, sat the haunted mansion, a dark silhouette against darker storm clouds. Beyond the

ancient iron fence at the far end of the park was the cemetery with its decaying tombstones. A small pool of brackish rainwater had collected beneath the fence, reflecting the black leafless trees over-head.

Her throat tight with terror, Sarah tried one last time to get her horse's attention.

"Please," she cried. But without slowing, Turbo headed straight for a spot on the iron fence to the right of where an ancient, twisted tree stretched toward the sky, looking like some kind of dark, monstrous skeleton just escaped from the grave. As the horse's hooves left the ground for the jump, Sarah looked down. Directly below her, she could see Turbo's reflection in the pool of rainwater under the fence. She caught a fleeting glimpse of her own terrified face, and beside it she saw Jake again, horrible and bloody and so real that his too-bright eyes seemed to take hold of her very soul.

Jake raised his arm. He was gesturing at some-thing urgently, pointing upward toward the tree.

And then, in a sudden flash, Sarah understood.

Instantly she ducked low, hugging her face to Turbo's hot neck. Her head just barely cleared the thick, deadly branch stretching out over the fence. She was so close that strands of her hair caught in the bark and tore loose. She flinched at the pain.

A few inches higher and her face would have smashed full force into the branch.

Somehow Turbo managed to land safely between two cracked and mossy headstones. Almost immediately he began to calm, responding at last to Sarah's soothing commands. She gathered up the flapping reins and pulled him to a halt. She dismounted and leaned against his warm, sweaty side for a moment while she waited for her legs to stop shaking. Then she led him back through the graves toward the fence.

Sarah remounted and reached for the branch overhanging the rusty fence. She stood up in the stirrups, balancing carefully, and searched the wood. There they were, almost completely grown over, and barely visible in the dim sunlight filtering through the storm clouds.

Two white teeth protruded from the bark.

Sarah shuddered. This was the tree that had killed Jake MacHeath—the tree that would have killed her, too, had it not been for Jake's warnings.

She stole a nervous glance at the haunted mansion. The windows were dark. Not a soul stirred inside.

Dismounting once again, Sarah knelt next to the

tombstone beneath the tree. Brushing away the dirt and mold, she could just make out the epitaph.

Sarah patted the top of the stone and smiled gently. "Thanks for the warning, Jake," she whispered.

# MUSIC TO THEIR EARS

If you don't stop playing that stupid horn, I'm going to twist it around your neck!"

Brandon Morrell lowered the clarinet from his mouth and glared at his brother Jeremy. Jeremy was only two years older than Brandon, but he was *much* bigger.

"I have a right to practice my clarinet," Brandon said.

"No you don't, Bran*dumb*," said Brandon's other brother, Rick. Rick was even bigger than Jeremy.

"Mom said you shouldn't call me that anymore," Brandon said.

"Well, Mom isn't here right now, Bran*dumb*," Rick pointed out. "So take your noise somewhere else. Jeremy and I are deciding what to be for Halloween, and that screeching horn is driving us crazy."

Brandon opened his mouth to argue further, but then he snapped it shut again. He knew it was pointless arguing with his brothers. The last time he'd tried it, they had picked him up, carried him to the bathroom, and started to stick his head in the toilet. Luckily their mother had come home just in time to save Brandon from the dunking—but he might not be so lucky again.

Brandon took his clarinet apart and laid it carefully in its velvet-lined case. He went outside, ignoring his brothers' triumphant grins, and headed down the street toward the park.

Sedgwick Park had been abandoned long ago. The benches were covered with graffiti. Ugly weeds poked through cracks in the cement walks. When the wind blew, it whistled through the gloomy old oak trees like the wailing of lost souls.

But it was the one place where Brandon could play his clarinet without being bothered. Almost no one went into Sedgwick Park during the day, and absolutely no one went there after dark. Not only was the park a shabby, depressing place, choked with weeds and litter, but it was located right next to the spooky old graveyard on the grounds of an abandoned mansion. But none of that bothered Brandon. It was quiet and it was private, and there were no brothers there to tease him about his music.

Brandon headed for his usual spot, a bench beside a stream now filled with garbage and weeds. Through the bars of a rusted iron fence, he could see the graveyard and the dilapidated old mansion beyond. Rick and Jeremy had told him spine-tingling tales about the mansion. They claimed it was haunted, but Brandon didn't believe a word of it. He was much too smart to believe in ghosts.

Brandon took out his clarinet and began to warm up. After playing a few scales, he started working on the piece they were learning in band. He wanted to get it just right before rehearsal next week.

He was so deep in concentration that he didn't even notice when the sun began to set. The tombstones in the graveyard cast long slender shadows toward the little park, and darkness crept out in ever-widening circles from beneath the trees. Still Brandon played on.

Suddenly he heard something—a strange, unearthly sound.

He stopped playing and listened. It couldn't have been, and yet . . . it had sounded like a musical instrument. Like a faraway trumpet, perhaps, calling through a thick fog.

"Just my imagination," Brandon told himself with a shrug.

He began to play again. This time, as soon as the first notes escaped his clarinet, the sound of the distant horn returned.

Brandon stopped. The trumpet stopped, too.

"Weird," Brandon whispered.

He started up again, listening carefully for his mysterious accompanist. The trumpet returned, but now it was joined by the deep notes of a bass. And the strangest thing was that they were both playing the same song Brandon was.

As he continued to play, Brandon stood on the bench and peered into the gloom. No one was in sight. His mind must be playing tricks on him. He furrowed his brow. That wasn't like him. He hadn't even had a nightmare since he was five years old.

He lowered his clarinet and glanced at his watch. He was going to be late for dinner. He put the instrument away and headed for home, still listening for the mysterious music. But it never returned.

The next afternoon when Brandon got home from school, he found the house empty. "Rick?" he called out. "Jeremy?"

There was no answer. Brandon breathed a sigh of relief. Good. For once he could play his clarinet in the house without having to worry about his brothers.

He sat down on the couch and took his clarinet from its case. He began a simple C-major scale.

"Aaaaargggghh!" A hideous creature, its face covered in bleeding sores, leaped from behind the couch, waving a bloody ax.

"Gggrrrrrraaaawwww!" A second creature, its eyes dangling from their sockets in oozing globs, burst from the closet, brandishing a butcher knife.

Brandon put down his clarinet. He shook his head. "You're both *so* funny," he said sarcastically.

Jeremy yanked off his mask. "You were scared. Admit it, Bran*dumb*."

"I saw you jump," Rick added hopefully.

"Why would I be scared?" Brandon asked. "You both look so much better than you usually do."

"What are *you* going to be for Halloween?" Jeremy asked. "Are you going to dress up as a geek? Oh, wait, I forgot—you *are* a geek."

Brandon returned his clarinet to its case and headed out the door. "I should have known," he muttered. "There's no way those two will ever let me practice in the house."

At Sedgwick Park he sat down on his usual bench. As he prepared to play, Brandon glanced over his shoulder. Would he hear the phantom instrumentalists again? Or had he just been imagining things the night before?

He began to play. This time the trumpet joined in right away. It still sounded far off in the distance, a sweet, muted sound, but he could hear it more clearly today.

"He's playing the same tune I am again," Brandon whispered. He tried a few more bars, and sure enough, the trumpet player was joined by a bassist. Seconds later a drummer picked up the beat.

Brandon stopped. Immediately all was quiet. He stood and looked around. Nothing. Just scraggly grass and ancient trees and the mossy stones of the graveyard across the fence.

"Where are you?" Brandon yelled.

Silence was the only answer.

Brandon began to play again, and once more the band joined in. It was excellent, he decided. Inspiring. He'd never played with such good musicians. When he switched to another tune, they followed him perfectly. Later, when the trumpet launched into a different song, Brandon was able to join right in.

It was the most fun he'd ever had. A dream come true. This was nothing like the pathetic school band, with its beginning players struggling to find the right note and keep the beat.

Here, he was part of a real band—a great band.

At last Brandon told himself he had to stop. He had never stayed this late in the park. If not for the light of the almost-full moon, he would have had a hard time finding his way out.

"I have to go," he yelled toward his unseen partners.

"Wait."

Brandon leaped a foot in the air. The voice was very near. He squinted into the darkness and saw an ancient-looking man standing in the cemetery, just beyond the graveyard fence.

"Hey, kid, you sure can jam on that horn," the man said.

"Thanks," Brandon said uneasily, fighting the impulse to run. For all he knew, this guy could be an ax murderer.

The man held up his trumpet for Brandon to see. "My name's Silas. We've been enjoying your sound, kid. How'd you like to play a gig with us?"

"A *real* gig?" Brandon knew that a gig was what musicians called a performance. "You mean, with a real audience? Not just a bunch of bored-looking parents?"

Silas smiled. He had terrible teeth, and his hair was wild and scraggly. "Yes, I can guarantee there'll be a real audience. See, we play this gig every year on the same night. Tomorrow night. It could be a big chance for you to show off what you can do."

"Tomorrow night is Halloween," Brandon pointed out.

"So it is," Silas said. He gave a soft laugh. "So it is. You in, kid? We sure could use you there."

Brandon hesitated. "I guess. Where . . . where do I go?"

"Just meet me right here," the man said. "At sunset."

All that night and the next day, Brandon spent every spare second wondering whether he should return to the park. There had definitely been something weird about Silas. But then, when would Brandon be offered another chance to play his clarinet with a real band, in front of a real live audience? How could he possibly pass up that kind of opportunity?

As dusk fell, Brandon left his house and headed toward the park. Luckily his mother had left early for the party she was attending, so she didn't ask where he was going. Rick and Jeremy had taken off a few minutes later—probably in a hurry to start terrorizing little kids, Brandon thought. Trick-or-treaters roamed the streets, dressed as ghosts and ghouls and vampires. But tonight Brandon had more important things to think about than costumes and candy—not to mention his idiot brothers. Instead of a costume, he'd donned a clean white shirt and a nice pair of pants. After all, it was important to look one's best in front of an audience.

The park was silent when he arrived. Brandon waited by the rusty iron fence, staring through it at the cold gray tombstones and wondering what his brothers would think if they knew he was here, at the haunted mansion, on Halloween night. As the black night crept in around him, he played a few warm-up scales, then ran through a couple of songs. The old gnarled oak at the edge of the graveyard seemed to sway in time to his music—but, of course, that had to be his imagination. There was no breeze.

Finally, just when Brandon was beginning to give up hope, Silas appeared on the other side of the fence. "Hey, there," he said. "You ready, kid? The other guys are waiting for us. Follow me."

Silas motioned Brandon to a gate in the fence. "Funny," Brandon said, "I've never noticed this before." He pushed on the gate, which opened with a loud, rusty shriek, and stepped into the graveyard.

"Some people would be scared being in a cemetery at night," Silas said, glancing at Brandon as he led him among the graves.

Brandon shrugged. "I guess so," he said. "But not me. I don't believe in ghosts." He nearly tripped over a cracked white headstone, catching himself just in time.

They passed row after row of moldering tombstones and crumbling mausoleums. The eyes of cold marble statues, shining in the silvery moonlight, seemed to follow their progress. But that, of course, was pure imagination.

In the center of the graveyard two other men, even shabbier than Silas, were waiting. One was holding a big bass fiddle. The other sat at a set of drums.

"Brandon, meet my pals. Skat's the one on drums, and Curt is on the bass there."

The two musicians raised thin, ragged hands in greeting.

"Let's jam," Curt said in a raspy voice.

"But . . . but . . . I thought there would be a stage," Brandon protested. "And an audience."

"Oh, there'll be an audience, all right," Skat said, cackling gleefully.

"Just play, kid," Silas said. "The audience will come. And let me give you one piece of advice. Once the audience shows up, don't *stop* playing. Do

40

you hear me? *Don't stop playing for anything!"*

Brandon swallowed hard. The old mansion loomed silently above them. Every horror story he'd ever heard about it came back to him now in terrifying detail. But those stories were ridiculous— weren't they?

Before he could say any more, the other three musicians began to play. Immediately Brandon forgot all about ghosts and haunted mansions. *This* was what he had come for—the music. He smiled and joined in, picking up the tune instantly. Never mind if Silas and his friends were a little shabby and odd looking—this was the kind of band Brandon had waited his whole life for. He could play with them forever.

They had just begun their second song when Brandon heard the sound of splintering wood and the squeal of rusty hinges.

And then, right in front of him, the ground began to move. Slowly it swelled. It bulged and throbbed as if something beneath it were trying to emerge.

Brandon gasped, nearly dropping his clarinet in terror.

"Don't stop!" Silas shrieked. "Don't stop!"

Faster and faster the music surged. Brandon's fingers flew as an icy terror grew inside him. But

even if he'd wanted to stop, he couldn't have. The music seemed to have taken over. The rhythm was more compelling than the frantic beat of his own heart. The melody wound a spell around him that he could not break.

Brandon watched, barely conscious of the notes he was playing, as the ground in front of each tombstone began to split. In the marble mausoleums nearby, doors were creaking open on rusty hinges.

A few feet away a long, white, bony hand emerged. A skeletal arm followed. Then the head of a skeleton popped out of the loose dirt and grinned up at the band.

A scream erupted from Brandon's lips.

"Don't stop playing, you fool! Not if you want to live!" Silas shouted.

Brandon played on. Played on, as all over the graveyard the skeletons crawled up out of the dirt. Some still wore the clothes they had been buried in, though the suits were now rotting away, the dresses slimy with worms and maggots.

Slowly the dead gathered around the band and began to dance. The brittle air was filled with the sounds of rattling bones and shrieks of unearthly delight.

Still Brandon played. He played until his fingers were numb and his mind was number. At last he could play no more. He let the clarinet fall from his lips.

Suddenly the nearest skeleton leaped at him. A cold bony claw, still slick with wet dirt, encircled his throat.

"Play!" Silas commanded. "Play or you'll be finished!"

With his last bit of energy, Brandon picked up his clarinet and began, somehow, to play again, while the moon rose high and the dead danced their gruesome dance.

He couldn't remember falling asleep, but he must have. He awoke, cold and numb, his back against a mossy tombstone.

The bloodred sun was just coming up behind the haunted mansion. Brandon gazed around the cemetery. There was no sign of the skeletons. The dead had disappeared back into their wet, dark tombs. The earth seemed undisturbed.

Maybe it had all been a horrible nightmare. Yes, Brandon thought, that would explain it. A Halloween nightmare and nothing more. He wasn't used to having nightmares—that could be why it had all seemed so real. Even down to his sore mouth and stiff fingers.

Then his eyes fell on the epitaph carved into a nearby gravestone.

Brandon shuddered. With trembling hands, he reached for his clarinet. Carefully he buried it in the moist soil beside Silas's grave.

"I think maybe I'll take up tennis instead," he murmured.

# THE EYES HAVE IT

I'm going in," Marnie McGee declared.

"No you're not," her little sister, Jenna, replied.

"Let me get this straight. Who is fifteen and who is ten, and who is in charge of who while Mom and Dad are away?"

"Whom," Jenna corrected. "And they'll be back from their high school reunion tomorrow, O incredibly bossy one, which means you don't get to lord it over me for much longer."

"If I'm going to have a modeling career, I need a portfolio," Marnie said. She stared again at the sign propped against the rusty old fence in front of them. *The Eyes Have It Photo Studio*, it read. *Look Your Very Best . . . Forever.*

"First of all, Mom said you couldn't even think

about modeling until you're seventeen," Jenna reminded her sister. "And second of all, why would anybody in their right mind open a photo studio in this creepy old house? It's haunted, you know." She shuddered as she looked at the dilapidated mansion at the end of the long, crooked walk.

"Haunted? Puh-leeze." Marnie tossed her shimmering blond hair. "The sign says they're having a grand opening special. See? *Free Glamour Photo.*"

"I still say this is a weird location for a photo studio," Jenna said. *"Really* weird."

Marnie pushed open the creaky gate and strode down the walk toward the gloomy old house. Jenna watched her, groaning inwardly. Marnie was bossy, obnoxious, and horribly vain. And those were her good points.

Still, she *was* Jenna's big sister. Jenna sighed and followed her.

Just as Marnie lifted her hand to ring the bell, the door swung open, as if someone had been awaiting her arrival. Marnie gasped at the woman who opened the door. Had there ever been an uglier old crone? It wasn't just the thin, greasy, white-haired bun. It wasn't just the hunched back, or the knotted, arthritic hands. It was the face. Skin the bluish white of skim milk. Tiny ratlike eyes. A hooked nose. Why, she even had warts. *Hairy* warts.

47

Her voice came as a surprise. It was as smooth and sweet as ice cream. "It is indeed my lucky day," she said, latching a bony hand onto Marnie's shoulder.

"Well, I—" Marnie hesitated. She had a very low tolerance for ugly people. She felt pity for them, of course. Not everyone could be born with her glorious looks. But still, they were so . . . well . . . so *unappetizing*.

"It would be an honor to capture that angelic face on film," said the woman in her silky voice. "Those eyes! Where did you get such eyes? The color of cornflowers, they are." She smiled, a strange, knowing smile. "I can make you more beautiful than you've ever dreamed, my dear."

"Well, I suppose it wouldn't hurt to take a few pictures," Marnie relented. "I'm starting a portfolio."

"My name is Aphton," said the old woman as she led the girls into a long, dark, cobweb-filled hallway.

"I'm Marnie McGee, and this is my sister, Jenna."

"Sister!" The woman peered at Jenna with her shiny rat eyes. "Ah, well, such is the luck of the draw, my dear. We can't all be blessed with the face of an angel, now can we? The world would be a dull place indeed if we all were so beautiful! And after all, you did get your sister's beautiful eyes. That's a comfort, at least."

48

Jenna cringed. It wasn't the first time she'd heard such a thing. *You must be adopted. I see who got the ugly genes.*

Aphton led the girls to a small, musty room. A large chair with a black velvet drape behind it sat against the far wall. In front of it was a big, complicated-looking camera on a tripod.

"Isn't this a wonderful location for a studio?" Aphton said. "The light is simply divine. And the view!"

"But there's a cemetery outside your window," Jenna said.

"Yes," said Aphton. "It makes for such quiet neighbors." She gazed out the window with a sigh. "Of course, I won't be here for long, but still, I'll enjoy the old place while I can."

"What do you mean?" Jenna asked.

Aphton gave a dismissive wave. "Nothing, dear. Just an old woman's ramblings."

"That's a weird camera," Marnie said as she fussed with her hair. "Is it an antique?"

"It's one of a kind," Aphton replied. "There's not another camera like it. It has a way of . . . revealing the real subject."

Jenna gazed at the long rows of photos covering the walls. Each one showed a person of unparalleled beauty. All had the most radiant smiles and exquisite features. And yet, as stunning as they all were, there was something . . . not quite right about the photos. They gave Jenna a twisting, uneasy feeling deep in her stomach, although she couldn't say why.

"There's something about these pictures," she muttered.

"Lovely, aren't they?" Aphton asked.

"I don't know what it is," Jenna said. "The eyes, maybe—"

"Ah yes." Aphton focused the camera on Marnie. "The eyes are windows to the soul, so they say."

"Is my hair okay, Jen?" Marnie asked anxiously.

"Don't worry yourself, dear," Aphton soothed. "The camera will make you more beautiful than you've ever dreamed."

"Like she's not vain enough already," Jenna muttered.

"I'm not vain," Marnie said. "I'm just aware of my assets." She flashed a smile at Aphton. "Did I mention that I'm going to be a model?"

"Don't wait too long," Aphton said. She stared out the window, sighing softly. "Beauty fades so quickly, my dear."

Jenna pointed to several smooth gray marble slabs in a corner. "What are those?" she asked, laughing uneasily. "If I didn't know better, I'd say they were tombstones."

"I sometimes find them necessary in my work," Aphton said.

"You mean, like . . . for props?" Jenna asked, but the old woman didn't answer. She pushed a button, a blinding flash filled the room, and the camera whirred to life.

"Wait a second," Marnie huffed. "I wasn't even posing. Do you have a fan? I was thinking we could do one of those windswept pictures with my hair flying, you know?"

"That won't be necessary," Aphton said as the camera spat out a large square instant-film cartridge. "We're through."

"Through?" Marnie cried. "What about my portfolio?"

"Quite through," Aphton repeated.

"I can pay you," Marnie pleaded. "I have money—"

"I'm not interested in your money," Aphton said curtly. "I am interested in capturing beauty on film."

"This stinks," Marnie fumed, marching over to Jenna. "One minute she's thrilled about my angel looks and my corny eyes—"

"Cornflower," Jenna corrected. She lowered her voice to a whisper. "I told you this was a dumb idea. Besides, don't these pictures give you the creeps? Check out the eyes."

Just then Aphton peeled away a layer on the instant film and let out a huge, plaintive sigh.

Marnie ran to see the photo. Her eyes went wide. "I knew I was pretty," she said, her voice hushed. "But this—"

"As I promised, it is a very special camera," said Aphton. She curled a bony finger at Jenna. "Come see your beautiful sister," she said with an eerie smile.

Jenna gasped at the gorgeous creature gazing up at her from the photo. Marnie's hair glinted like spun gold, and her skin glowed as pink and perfect as a dawn sky. But it was her eyes that riveted Jenna, sparkling with life and spirit, very nearly real.

"Can you do that to me?" Jenna asked shyly.

"I'm afraid not, my dear," Aphton said. "I save my skills for only a select few."

Jenna bit her lip and looked down. It had been a stupid thing to ask. Even if she did have the same pretty blue eyes as Marnie—those sparkling cornflower blue eyes—no photo would ever make her look like her sister. She knew that. Still, Aphton didn't have to be so blunt about it.

Marnie reached for the photo. "I know the sign said the first photo is free, but I really want to pay you something. After all, this picture could be my ticket to a modeling career."

Aphton snatched the picture back. "Impossible,"

she snapped. "This photo is for my collection."

"But you can't keep it!" Marnie wailed. "That's a picture of *me*. It belongs to *me*. It *is* me!"

"You're quite mistaken, my dear," said Aphton darkly. "The photo belongs to me, and it always will."

Marnie gazed at the photo longingly. "I'll pay you," she pleaded. "Just tell me how much. I'll pay you anything."

Aphton waved a gnarled finger at her. "Ah, but you can't put a price on beauty, my dear," she said, and then she shuffled away, cackling softly to herself.

When their parents called to check on them that evening, the girls made no mention of the visit to Aphton's studio. Jenna had been tempted to tell on her big sister, but Marnie was so upset about the photo that Jenna decided against it.

Working on homework that night in the room they shared, Marnie was strangely quiet. "Are you okay?" Jenna asked.

Marnie looked up from her math assignment. "I don't know. It's weird. I feel sort of dizzy. You know—light-headed."

"You do look a little pale," Jenna said. "Maybe you're getting sick."

"No. It's that photo," Marnie said. "I know it

sounds crazy, but I've never wanted anything so much in my whole life. I can't think about anything else."

"Well, it *was* beautiful," Jenna said, feeling a twinge of resentment.

"You mean *I* was beautiful in it," Marnie corrected. "It wasn't just that, though. I felt like I was leaving a part of myself behind, you know?"

Jenna thought again of the strange, unsettling photos lining Aphton's walls. "Well, I wouldn't worry," she said. "What's one picture, anyway?"

In the middle of the night Jenna awoke. Pale yellow light from a full moon poured over the floor. She turned to check on Marnie. The bed was empty.

Suddenly the bedroom door creaked open, inch by inch. "Marnie?" Jenna whispered.

Marnie slipped through the door. She was wearing her thick terry-cloth robe. A towel was draped over her head.

"What are you doing? Washing your hair in the middle of the night?" Jenna demanded.

"Jen," Marnie whispered. "Something's *happening* to me."

The fear in her sister's voice made Jenna sit straight up in bed. "Stop kidding around. It's two in the morning."

54

Slowly, very slowly, Marnie walked to the center of the room. She stood in a pool of moonlight. Then she kicked off her slippers and untied the belt of her robe.

"This is no time for a fashion show," Jenna tried to joke.

Suddenly Marnie dropped her robe to the floor and whipped the towel off her head. She was wearing the faded old football jersey she always wore to bed. The gold shirt caught the moonlight faintly.

But the rest of the moonlight shot right through her.

"Marnie!" Jenna cried in horror. Her sister was there, standing right in front of her—or was she? Marnie's skin had a ghostly translucence. Staring at her sister, Jenna could make out the dresser behind her, the poster on the wall, the chair. It was like peering through fog.

"I'm fading," Marnie whimpered. She held out her trembling hand to Jenna.

Jenna reached out to grab it. She touched something cold and damp, like a cold mist against her skin, but that was all.

All night Jenna sat with her sister, watching as the color seemed to seep from Marnie's body. By 5:00 A.M., Marnie was nothing more than a shadow. Her

features were barely visible, and even her voice had grown muted and soft around the edges.

"Where are we going?" Marnie asked weakly as Jenna tied a scarf around her sister's head.

"We're going back to the haunted mansion," Jenna said angrily. "Back to see Aphton."

"Make her give me my picture," Marnie whispered. "I want my picture. . . ."

Dressed in a bulky sweater, gloves, and pants, Marnie almost looked normal—that is, until Jenna tried to meet her eyes. They were just a blue glimmer, blurred like a reflection in a foggy mirror. Instead of bright cornflower, Marnie's eyes were now the pale, pale blue of frost on a windowpane.

Night still shrouded the town, and the girls met no one as they walked. Jenna shuddered as she led her sister past Sedgwick Park and the haunted mansion loomed into view.

The door to the mansion opened before Jenna could knock. Aphton was wearing a gray nightdress and carrying a candle. She didn't seem at all surprised to see them.

"What have you done to Marnie?" Jenna demanded, storming into the shadowy hall.

Aphton peered at Marnie, a dark look on her ugly face. "My, my, you do look a little pale, Marnie," she said.

Jenna grabbed the woman's bony arm. "This has something to do with that photo you took, doesn't it? You've got to do something!"

"The photo." Aphton smiled a private smile. "Come. You must see it."

She pulled free of Jenna's grip and led the girls to her studio. In the early-morning darkness, flickering candles threw huge leaping shadows against the walls. "I couldn't wait to frame it," Aphton whispered.

Jenna and Marnie stared at the picture on the wall. It was Marnie's photo. But somehow it was something more.

"It's . . . it's even more beautiful," Marnie said.

It was true. The girl in the photograph was radiant. But it was her eyes that mesmerized Jenna. The impossibly blue eyes that seemed to follow her as she moved.

The eyes that seemed alive.

"You've got to destroy that photo," Jenna said, fighting back the icy fear clutching at her heart.

"No!" Marnie said desperately, seizing the photo.

"But it's killing you, can't you see that?" Jenna cried. "Somehow it's sapping the life right out of you."

The ghostly mist that was Marnie clutched at the picture. "We can't destroy something of such beauty.

I've never . . ." Her voice faded. "I've never been so beautiful."

"Marnie," Jenna pleaded, "you don't have much longer."

"She understands," Aphton said. "Don't you, Marnie? Beauty fades. But a picture—why, a picture lasts forever."

"Give me the picture," Jenna commanded. She lunged for the photo, but Marnie's grip was deathly tight. Jenna pulled at her sister's arm, but it was like trying to hold on to air.

How could her sister hold so tight when her very flesh was nothing more than mist?

"You cannot take it from her, Jenna," Aphton said, as if reading her mind. "Don't you see? She holds it with a force greater than anything merely physical. She is holding on to it with the sheer force of her vanity!" Aphton cackled as the candles cast craggy shadows over her withered, hideous face. "Can't you see that this is how it must be? The vain must learn that beauty does not last."

Frantically Jenna ran to the camera in the middle of the room. She turned it on Aphton, fumbling to locate the controls. At last she found the right button, and the camera whirred into action with a blinding flash.

Jenna yanked the instant-film cartridge from the

camera. "Now," she cried triumphantly, holding the film high, "release Marnie or I'll never let you have your own picture. You'll suffer the same fate!"

Aphton threw back her head and howled. "Go ahead," she said. "Go ahead and see your handi-work!"

Her hands shaking violently, Jenna peeled the cover off the instant film.

The room was there, the photos on the wall, the slight blur of the candles.

But Aphton was nowhere to be seen.

"The camera only works on the vain, you fool," Aphton cried with a bitter laugh. "It doesn't work on people like you or me. Only on those to whom beauty is more important than life itself—those like your sister!"

Suddenly there was a thud. Jenna spun around to see Marnie's photograph on the floor. Next to it lay a heap of clothing.

Marnie had vanished.

"She's gone!" Jenna sobbed in horror. "She's gone!"

Calmly Aphton returned the photo to the wall. "Such a lovely girl," she murmured. "And those eyes! Bluer than cornflowers, I tell you."

Jenna turned to the photo of her sister. The beautiful blue eyes gazed back at Jenna. She couldn't be sure, but they seemed to be filled with tears.

■        ■        ■

Later that day Jenna watched, sobbing softly, as two police officers pounded on the front door of the haunted mansion.

"Aphton's in there," Jenna said as her mother wrapped a comforting arm around her shoulder. "I'm telling you she's in there."

"No one seems to be answering, miss," said one of the officers, a young man with a wispy mustache.

"Then break down the door if you have to," Jenna's father exploded, fists clenched with rage. "My daughter is missing, and if you don't break in, I will!"

The second officer, an older, balding man, reached for the door handle. But before he could touch it, the door swung open with a low moan.

Cautiously, the policemen stepped inside. "Wait here, folks," the younger one said, but Jenna rushed past them into Aphton's studio.

Her footsteps echoed loudly in the empty room. The walls were completely bare. "But . . . but there were pictures on the wall. I swear there were," Jenna cried. "With these weird eyes that followed you everywhere. And there was a camera over there, and . . ." Her voice evaporated.

There, on the floor, lay a pile of clothes. Marnie's clothes. They looked solid and real, not half-transparent as they had when Marnie was wearing them.

Jenna's mother saw them and fell to the floor. Her face buried in Marnie's sweater, she began to sob uncontrollably.

"No sign of the old woman," the younger policeman reported. "The place looks abandoned if you ask me."

Suddenly Jenna froze, her eyes locked on something just outside the window. The new gravestone glittered cruelly in the afternoon sun.

"Marnie, honey," Jenna's mother sobbed. "Where are you?"

"I think I know, Mom," Jenna whispered as she read the fresh inscription in the gray marble.

IN MEMORIAM
MARNIE McGEE
CAPTURED ON FILM
FOR ETERNITY

# LATE FOR THE WEDDING

A lex Little hated wearing a suit.

Unfortunately, for the last three hours, thirty-seven minutes, and sixteen seconds, he'd been wearing one.

First he'd had to sit through the funeral of his great-great-uncle Caleb, chafing under the stiff collar of the new shirt his mother had bought for the occasion. And now here he was, standing in this extremely creepy cemetery, sweating in the eighty-degree sun.

He'd told his parents he didn't want to come. He had never even met his great-great-uncle Caleb. He'd heard stories about the old man, of course, at family get-togethers. And from what he'd heard, Caleb hadn't exactly been the nicest guy on the planet.

Of course, you could tell that just from looking at

the house Caleb had once lived in. Everyone said the mansion was haunted, and who was Alex to argue? It sure looked haunted, with its gray, run-down exterior and overgrown lawn. Besides, it had its very own cemetery—not exactly a good sign. Caleb had moved away to a warmer climate long ago—before Alex's parents were born—but he'd asked to be buried here, next to the house he'd loved.

Alex glanced over his shoulder at the mansion. Even on a sunny afternoon like this, the place was enough to give someone the shivers.

He watched as Caleb's coffin was slowly lowered into the wet black grave. Here and there a mourner sniffled while the minister spoke in hushed tones.

A man standing near the foot of the grave caught Alex's eye. He was tall and gaunt and very old. His battered black hat and weather-beaten face seemed to come from another time and place. As the coffin settled at the bottom of the grave, the man suddenly let out a loud, satisfied laugh.

Other mourners turned to stare in disbelief at the man's poor taste. But the man didn't seem to care. He hobbled to a nearby headstone. Unlike the other stones, this one was new, glistening in the dappled sun. Gently the man placed a single red rose on the grave. Then he slowly walked away.

64

Alex squinted to see the inscription on the head-stone.

HERE LIES
SALLY LITTLE

BUT HER SPIRIT
WILL NOT REST
UNTIL SHE'S REUNITED
WITH THE ONE
WHO LOVED HER BEST

Sally Little. Alex had never heard the name before, but then, there were plenty of far-flung members of the Little clan he'd never heard of. He just hoped he wouldn't have to attend all *their* funerals, too.

After the burial, people milled about, murmuring comforting words to one another. Alex wandered away from the crowd and leaned against the rusty iron fence surrounding the graveyard to wait for his parents. He knew it would probably be a long wait. His mother and father ran a florist shop called A Little Something Special, and they had provided most of the flower arrangements for Caleb's funeral. They were already mobbed with people thanking them for the fine work they'd done.

It had always struck Alex as a little ghoulish the way his family made money off other people's tragedies—deaths and sickness. Of course, his mother always reminded him, they also did flowers for happy occasions such as birthdays and weddings. In any case, Alex didn't mind. He worked as a delivery boy for the shop after school and on weekends. The town wasn't very large, and he could carry most small arrangements on his bike. The tips were great.

Alex yanked off his tie, took off his jacket, and rolled up his sleeves, feeling the sun soak into his back. With his eyes closed, he could almost pretend he was lying on a beach somewhere instead of standing in the middle of an eerie, untended graveyard.

"Lovely day for a funeral, eh?"

Startled, Alex opened his eyes to see the tall old man he'd noticed earlier.

"I guess," Alex said. He shrugged. "Man, I hate suits."

The man chuckled. "Get no argument from me there. I'm a farmer myself. Give me a pair of overalls and I'm a happy man." He extended a hand and Alex shook it. The bony fingers were thickly calloused. "John O'Hannon. I hear tell you're Jacob Little's son. Alex, is it?"

Alex nodded.

"That would make Caleb your great-great-uncle?"

"Well, I never met him or anything."

John smiled grimly. "Count that as a blessing, my boy."

"Did you know him?" Alex asked. "I've heard he was kind of a jerk."

"A jerk?" John savored the word, as if he'd never tried it out before. "In my day we called a man like him a scoundrel, a cur—" His voice rose, and he seemed to struggle to control it. "*Wicked.* Yes, that's the word for Caleb Little. The only word. *Wicked* through and through."

"What did he do?" Alex asked, intrigued.

"See that headstone over yonder? The one with the red rose?" John's milky blue eyes softened. "That's your great-great-uncle Caleb's only child, Sally. She died fifty years ago, a mere girl, at that. Nineteen she was, and the prettiest thing you ever did see." John smiled, a smile so wistful and faraway that he seemed to have forgotten Alex altogether. "Ah, how I loved that girl," he whispered.

Alex thought of the inscription on Sally's gravestone. Was John "the one who loved her best"?

"I asked Sally to marry me," John continued, his voice hardening. "But Caleb Little, no, Caleb would have none of that. He was a wealthy man, and I was a poor dirt farmer. No land, no future to speak of. I wasn't good enough for his Sally." He clenched his fists. "We decided to elope, Sally and me. We headed to the justice of the peace one county over. Late at night it was, and dark as pitch."

Suddenly John fell silent. He wiped a sleeve over his eyes in an awkward, embarrassed movement.

"What happened then?" Alex asked softly. He could see his parents motioning for him to join them, but he wanted to hear the end of the story. Usually he hated mushy romantic stuff, but something about John's story had him hooked.

"Caleb found out about us," John said. "He was a powerful man, and he had powerful contacts. He stopped the justice from marrying us, and he had me driven out of the state. Laid a curse on us, he did. Said as long as he lived, Sally and I would never marry." He cleared his throat. "Sally died a week later. Doc said her heart just plain gave out, but I knew better. It was broken." John turned his gaze to Caleb's grave. "He broke it," he whispered. "Caleb moved away from the mansion right after Sally died. I figure he couldn't take the guilt." He pointed to Sally's headstone. "I had that stone placed there the minute I heard old Caleb had finally kicked the bucket. The stone Caleb gave her just had her name and nothing more. This one tells the truth of it." He gave an odd, unsettling smile. "And I've got another one all prepared."

"Another one?" Alex repeated uneasily.

"Another gravestone," the old man replied.

Alex wondered what he meant but decided not to ask. There was something about John, something that made Alex not want to ask too many questions. "Well, I'd better shove off," he said quickly. "Nice talking to you. I'm, uh, you know . . . sorry things didn't work out with Sally. I mean, I kind of feel responsible in a dumb sort of way. Caleb was a relative and all."

"Wait." John latched a hand on Alex's shoulder. His grip was surprisingly strong for such an old man. "There is something you can do for me. Your parents own the florist shop on Sycamore Street, don't they?"

Alex nodded.

"Bring me a dozen red roses tomorrow at noon. Here, at the mansion. Can you do that for me, boy?"

"Sure. Roses are kind of expensive, though."

"Money is no object, not now," said John. He pressed several crisp bills into Alex's palm. The faraway look had returned to John's eyes. "Sally loves red roses."

"Okay then," Alex said, slipping from the old man's grip.

"Noon!" John called after him. "Don't be late, my boy. I've waited plenty long enough!"

Alex checked his watch as he rode toward the haunted mansion the next day. Eleven-fifty. Plenty of time. Unless, of course, the weather interfered.

When he'd left his parents' shop, the sky had been perfectly clear. Now, halfway to his destination, a huge bank of clouds was unfurling across the sky like a thick gray carpet. The sun had vanished, and the wind had picked up. Alex had to pedal hard to make any headway at all.

As the first cold drops of rain splashed on his arms, Alex glanced behind him at the custom-made bike basket in which he stored arrangements. The box of red roses was fine. He thought, not for the first time, about what John had said yesterday. *Sally loves red roses*, he'd said. Not *loved*. *Loves*.

A slip of the tongue, Alex's mother had assured him as she'd prepared the roses that morning. People often talked about loved ones who had passed on as if they were still alive.

"But she's been dead for fifty years," Alex had pointed out.

His mother had smiled at him. "You're too young to understand, hon," she'd said in her someday-you'll-get-it tone. "Love has a way of never dying."

Maybe so, Alex thought as he passed Sedgwick Park and the mansion towered into view. But he still had major creeps about delivering flowers to a place that looked like something out of a horror movie.

A brilliant bolt of lightning slashed the sky as Alex pulled up to the mansion. In a front window a single candle flickered. The rain was coming faster and harder now. Thick, roiling clouds had doused the sun.

Alex grabbed the flowers and dropped his bike by the gate. Suddenly another bolt of lightning split the clouds, and the rain came pouring down in icy torrents. Alex sprinted toward the mansion, barely noticing the graveyard as he passed it. If he didn't hurry, the cardboard flower box would be ruined. He'd have to go back to the shop and start all over again. And there was no way he wanted to make this trip twice.

Halfway to the mansion door, something made Alex stop. He froze, the rain pelting him, the box soggy in his arms. Slowly he looked back to the graveyard where he'd stood yesterday watching Caleb being lowered into the ground.

It was dark, almost as dark as night. Alex squint-ed, waiting for another round of lightning. Suddenly the sky was rent by a searing white flash, and he could see the graveyard clearly. Sally's rain-slicked headstone was no longer marking a grave.

It was marking a huge, gaping, freshly dug hole.

The box of flowers slipped from Alex's grasp. He stared, transfixed, at the empty grave now shrouded again in darkness. Another flash of lightning lit up the sky, and Alex could make out the rotting remains of a wooden coffin.

It was empty.

The flowers forgotten, Alex spun around. He had to leave this place. There was something terribly wrong here. But he couldn't move. Something was holding him by the shoulder in a viselike grip.

"Thanks for bringing the flowers. But you can't leave now," said a familiar voice. "We need a witness, my boy."

The grip loosened and Alex turned. John was dressed in an old, frayed tuxedo. A wilting red rose hung limply from a buttonhole.

"I . . . I can't stay, I have to go," Alex cried, his voice shaking uncontrollably.

"But she's waiting," John insisted. He pointed to the window where the candle still flickered faintly.

Alex followed his gaze. There was now something else visible beside the candle. Even through the curtain of torrential rain, Alex could make out a glow, a faint red glow the size of an open rose. It seemed to hang in the window, floating in the air.

"It's almost noon," John whispered. "Come."

Alex tried to run, but John grabbed his arm. How could such an old man be so strong? Alex wondered frantically.

"The grave," Alex choked. "Sally's grave—"

"Hurry now," John urged, swooping down to grab the wet box of roses from the ground. "We mustn't be late."

Up the wet front steps and into the bleak mouth of the mansion John dragged Alex. From an open door halfway down the narrow hall, a red light pulsed like a neon sign.

"No!" Alex cried. He grabbed at the door frame, trying to slow their progress, but his rain-slicked hands couldn't get a grip.

"But we need a witness, my boy," John repeated excitedly. "Come now. We've waited this long."

"I don't want to be a witness!" Alex screamed. "I don't want to—"

But it was too late. John dragged him the last few feet to the open door.

"Sally," John said, "meet Alex."

Alex stared in terror as John's bride, dressed in a torn and yellowed wedding gown, turned to smile— a bony, horrifying smile.

"She's . . . ," Alex whispered in terror, "she's a skeleton!"

John released Alex and opened the box of roses.

Gently he handed them to Sally. The bloodred flowers perfectly matched the glowing red heart beating steadily and hopefully beneath Sally's sheer gown.

Alex spun around and ran. Stumbling out of the mansion into the raging storm, forgetting all about his bike, he ran blindly, unable to see through the rain, conscious only of his own frantically beating heart.

He ran until he hit something, bruising his leg so hard that he cried out in pain. It was the fence around the cemetery.

Lightning pulsed in the black sky, and suddenly a new gravestone was revealed to him—a stone at the head of Sally's open, empty grave.

R I P

HERE'S WHERE SALLY LITTLE LAY
FOR WHAT SEEMED LIKE FOREVER.
SAID SALLY, ON HER WEDDING DAY,
'IT'S BETTER LATE THAN NEVER!'